Julia's House Moves On

This book is dedicated to my sweet Ida.
Forever and Always.

Copyright © 2020 by Ben Hatke

Published by First Second
First Second is an imprint of Roaring Brook Press,
a division of Holtzbrinck Publishing Holdings Limited Partnership
120 Broadway, New York, NY 10271

Don't miss your next favorite book from First Second!
For the latest updates go to firstsecondnewsletter.com and sign up for our enewsletter.

Library of Congress Control Number: 2019948197

ISBN: 978-1-250-19137-3

Our books may be purchased in bulk for promotional, educational, or business use.
Please contact your local bookseller or the Macmillan Corporate and Premium Sales
Department at (800) 221-7945 ext. 5442 or by email at MacmillanSpecialMarkets@macmillan.com.

First edition, 2020
Edited by Calista Brill and Kiara Valdez
Jacket design by Ben Hatke and Kirk Benshoff
Interior design by Kirk Benshoff
Printed in China by RR Donnelley Asia Printing Solutions Ltd.,
Dongguan City, Guangdong Province

10 9 8 7 6 5 4 3 2 1

Julia's House was for lost creatures of every kind.

But the house was getting restless. It was time to move on. Everyone could feel it.

The goblins were cranky and full of mischief.

The mermaid spent her days in languid sighs.

The ghost had faded, and the trolls just stared out the windows while reciting poems.

Yes, it was time to move on.

"I have a plan for this," said Julia.

She really did.

Books were packed.
Boxes stacked.
She had a nice spot picked
out in the mountains.

But
THEN...

... the house started moving on its own!

"HEY!"

shouted Julia.

"Where are you going?
This wasn't part of the PLAN!"

But the turtle didn't
care about the plan.

Not at all.

The tattered remains of Julia's House drifted on a lonely sea.

Things looked bleak.

The creatures sloshed about in the water, and they looked to Julia.

"Don't worry," she said. "I have a plan for this."

She really did.

"KICK!" shouted Julia. "FASTER!"

The creatures kicked as fast as they could.
The house listed dangerously to one side.

And then the goblins spotted
fins circling in the water.

The creatures scrambled back on board. The house was sinking faster.

"DON'T WORRY!" Julia called.

"I HAVE A PLAN FOR THIS!"

She ran to her workshop.
She tore through her boxes.

She sounded
Triton's Horn.

When the kraken sank below the waves, things were worse than ever. The creatures looked to one another.

"I can make a plan for this," whispered Julia.

Julia ran to her workshop. But when she emerged, the creatures were paddling to the horizon.

Julia was alone with her plan.

Julia stared out over the lonely sea. She opened her hand and watched her plans float away on the wind.

But THEN . . .

. . . the sea erupted in light and song!

The Queen of the Sea lifted Julia's House up, up out of the water.

The creatures were all there.

"We have a plan for this," they said.

They really did.

The goblins hammered and the robots wired. The ghost collected sheets and blankets.

And the ghillie—

The ghillie GREW,

Julia's House set a course
through the clouds.

The way ahead was uncertain, and it was
anyone's guess where they would land.

Julia was all out of plans.

And that was okay.